In loving memory of
Maguerite Ott Wagner

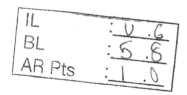

HOT LINE

Stress

by Laurie Beckelman

Series Consultant
John Livingstone, M.D.

Crestwood House
New York

Maxwell Macmillan Canada
Toronto

Maxwell Macmillan International
New York   Oxford   Singapore   Sydney

For my parents,
with love and gratitude

Author's Note:
Many teenagers generously shared their thoughts and experiences with me.
The quotes in this book are based on their stories.

Copyright © 1994 Crestwood House, Macmillan Publishing Company

Crestwood House
Macmillan Publishing Company
866 Third Avenue, New York, NY 10022

Maxwell Macmillan Canada, Inc.
1200 Eglinton Avenue East, Suite 200
Don Mills, Ontario M3C 3N1

Macmillan Publishing Company is part of the
Maxwell Communication Group of Companies.

First Edition
Design: Lynda Fishbourne, Hemenway Design Associates
Packaging: Prentice Associates Inc.
Photos:
Image Bank: Cover, 4, 22, 27, 37, Photo Edit: (David Young-Wolff) 10, 14, 34, 46, (Tony Freeman) 16, (Myrleen Ferguson Cate) 19, (Richard Hutchings) 24, (Bill Aron) 28, (Mary Kate Denny) 33, (Michael Newman) 42.

Printed in the United States of America
10 9 8 7 6 5 4 3 2 1

Library of Congress Cataloging-in-Publication Data
Beckelman, Laurie.
Stress / by Laurie Beckelman.— 1st ed.
p. cm. — (Hot line)
Includes bibliographical references and index.
ISBN 0-89686-848-6
1. Stress—Juvenile literature. 2. Stress in children. 3. Stress management—Juvenile literature. I. Title. II. Series.
BF575.S75B34 1994
155.9'042—dc20
0-382-24746-9 (pbk.)
94-2735

Summary: A discussion of stress and how it affects the body, relationships, and self-esteem. Provides examples of typical pressures in teenagers' lives and offers suggestions for managing stress effectively.

HOT LINE

Stress

CONTENTS

Family, teachers, friends— sometimes we feel like escaping them all. We have too many people pulling us in too many directions.

Living on Red Alert

Pressure. Sometimes it seems to come from everywhere . . .

Take out the garbage. Clean up your room. Where are you going? You're not leaving the house looking like that! No, you can't go to the party. I need you to baby-sit. We know you can make the team . . . get an A . . . practice harder . . . lose that weight . . .

What's the answer? Where's your homework? Quiet in the halls! Quiet in class! This is the last time I'm going to warn you. Your book reports are due Wednesday. Read Chapter 10 by Wednesday. Science exam Wednesday. Math quiz Wednesday. Civics test Wednesday.

Come on . . . you know you really want to. Hey, man, don't be like that. We're just having fun. Try it. Just a little won't hurt. No one will find out. You're inviting *Sally*? She's a nerd! If you were really my friend . . .

Family, teachers, friends—sometimes we feel like escaping them all. We have too many people pulling us in too many directions. Too much to do. Too much worry, too much doubt—too much **stress**!

Stress is the extra feeling we get when other emotions, pressure, or expectations seem like more than we can handle. When we're stressed, we may feel panicked, overwhelmed, or scared. We may get headaches, grind our teeth, bite our nails, or nervously tap our feet. We may feel as if everyone's demanding too much of us— as if everything's just too much.

We all face demands. These may be as ordinary as homework or as uncommon as adjusting to a friend's death. They may come from other people in our lives— like a parent who insists that we help clean the house— or from ourselves. For example, we may expect to be the top scorer on the soccer team, or we may set a goal to lose five pounds by a certain date.

Most often, the demands in our lives are not overly stressful. But they can be. When we have too much to do or when we doubt our ability to respond to a particular situation, we can become stressed out. So, too, when demands are conflicting. "I have two best friends, but they hate each other," explains Laura. "If one's over and the other calls, I never know what to do. I feel so torn." Laura sometimes feels as if she has to choose between two people she really likes. It's a very uncomfortable, and stressful, feeling.

Laura's stress is not necessarily harmful to her. It draws attention to a conflict in her life that she needs to resolve. If Laura sees her stress as a warning and a challenge, she can turn it to her advantage. It can prompt her to come up with creative solutions to her problem. It can help her grow.

Jeremy also learned that stress can be helpful. He made the discovery after he was selected to play a solo at his school's spring concert. "I was so nervous at first that I almost backed out. I was afraid I couldn't do it. But I really wanted to, so I backed out of some other things instead," he recalls. "I paid my kid brother to do my chores, and I convinced my mom to let me skip religious school a couple of times so I could practice. I practiced for hours. When the time came, I was really ready."

Learning to see stress as a warning and a challenge isn't easy, but you can do it. Since the 1970s, researchers have studied why some people thrive in stressful situations while others crumble. These investigators learned a lot from the people they studied. And you can benefit from what they found out. This book shares insights, tips, and techniques that can help you make stress an ally in the battle to be the best you can.

Why Care About Stress?

"Everyone feels stressed out sometimes," says Diana. "So what's the big deal?"

Diana's question is a good one. If we all experience stress—and we do—why should we worry about it? The answer has two parts.

The first has to do with your mind. Stress can suck the pleasure out of life. It can kill relaxation and crowd out thoughts of anything other than the problems causing your dismay. Says Sherri: "The other day? I had this really big science test to study for? But I also had soccer practice, and it was my grandma's birthday, so all my cousins and everyone were coming over and I had to help clean the house. I had no, I mean *no*, time to study. I was so stressed out about the test, I couldn't enjoy the party. All I kept thinking was, 'I'm gonna fail for sure. Then my dad will ground me.' It was really awful."

Stress can make us feel burdened, or cheated out of the pleasure we deserve. It can interfere not only with our delight in life but also with our ability to carry on. Andy had a math teacher who terrorized him. Andy felt that the teacher humiliated him in front of the other kids, gave him meaningless makeup work, and constantly told him that he was going to fail. Andy was so stressed out by his teacher's treatment that he was tongue-tied in class, which made matters worse. Homework that used to seem easy suddenly became hard because Andy couldn't concentrate. He began thinking that his teacher was right: He was a failure. He felt so humiliated that he didn't want to tell anyone about his problem. He kept it bottled up, and the pain and the stress kept growing.

The stress Andy felt began to affect his body. He started to get stomach cramps before class. Andy's discomfort illustrates the second reason for being concerned about stress: Intense stress that lasts a long time can damage the health of both body and mind.

Stress mobilizes what researcher Hans Selye called the **general adaptation response**. This is a one-size-fits-all response to any extra demand on the

Stress can make us feel burdened, or cheated out of the pleasure we deserve

body. When your body feels stress, your brain releases special chemicals that prepare you for physical action. Muscles tense. Heart rate increases. Digestion shuts off. Attention focuses. Energy increases.

The general adaptation response evolved millions of years ago to help our cave-dwelling ancestors fight off or flee from the very real physical threats in their world. But today's **stressors** are rarely like the ones that confronted our ancestors—a vicious math teacher poses a very different threat from a saber-toothed tiger. Since we can rarely solve our problems by fighting or fleeing, our bodies are ready for the wrong battle.

What's more, today's stressors come from many sources. We may be on almost constant alert. Says Tanika: "I avoid the drug dealers who hang near the bus stop by waiting inside 'til I can see the school bus coming. But then, once I get to school, I worry about staying clear of the gangs. And then there's my work."

When our bodies stay on alert for long periods of time, we can suffer health problems. Research shows that **stress hormones** make the **immune system** function less well. This makes us more vulnerable to infectious diseases, such as the flu and colds. Headaches, stomach problems, nervous tension, and heart disease have also been linked to stress.

So managing stress is important. You can learn to relax your body when you are stressed. You can learn, too, to use the energy the general adaptation response makes available to help rather than harm you. The first step is to understand what makes you feel stressed to begin with.

Life in the Teenage Lane

Diana: My parents won't let me date. Can you believe that? I lost a really good friend because of it. He asked me out, and I'd die before I'd tell him that I couldn't go because my parents won't let me, so I just said that I had other plans. Then he asked me again, and I had to make up another excuse. So now he hardly talks to me, and I really like him. What am I supposed to do?

Michael: I play the what-if game a lot. Like, what if my band really makes it? I see all the good times—the tours, the fans . . . man, it's great! But then, I also do the what-if-I-can't-get-a-job thing. What if I don't graduate? What if I can't help support my mom, who needs help bad? What if? What if? What if? This may sound weird, but sometimes I get worn out just from thinking.

Sherri: My mom's always getting on me about my clothes. She goes, like, 'Why don't you wear that nice sweater I bought you? Why don't you wear this? Why don't you wear that?' Doesn't she know that those clothes are *embarrassing*? I've got the biggest breasts of any girl in my class. The *only* thing I can wear are my sweatshirts! I mean, she didn't have this problem. She's always telling me how lucky I am to 'be built.' *Lucky?* Yeah, right.

The conflicts and concerns that Diana, Michael, and Sherri voice may sound familiar to you. They all reflect pressures that are common during the teen years. Like Diana, you might find that your parents' and your friends' expectations conflict with one another. You might be torn between two sets of values, two sets of ideas of how you should live your life. And adding to the stress may be several questions: Are *any* of their ideas right for you? What do *you* think? What do *you* believe? How can you hear your own ideas amid the clamor of other people's expectations and demands?

Like Michael, you might wonder a lot about the future. You are now capable of what **psychologist** David Elkind calls "thinking in a new key." You can imagine the future and foresee the consequences of actions in ways you simply could not as a child. Your

Talking to friends or trusted adults can also help. They may be able to help you sort out your feelings and fears.

new mental powers can help protect you against becoming overwhelmed by stress. They help you more realistically assess the pressures you face and better prepare to meet them.

But your new powers of mind can also contribute to stress. Because you can imagine what you want to do with your life, you may worry that you won't be able to fulfill your dreams. Or you may worry about what you will do with your life. You may find that problems beyond your control (for example, unemployment, global warming, the threat of nuclear war) become more understandable—and more threatening. You may, like Michael, become exhausted by all the new thinking you're doing.

And, like Sherri, you may worry about your body. It's changing, or will change soon, and the changes may not feel comfortable. You may worry about looking different from your friends or about being unattractive.

All of these concerns and conflicts are normal, and all of them can contribute to feelings of stress. When changes pile up, as they do in adolescence, stress can build even more. This is especially true when everyday pressures or important events in your life add to the load.

Sometimes just knowing that your feelings are normal helps you feel less overwhelmed and helpless. Talking to friends or trusted adults can also help. They may be able to help you sort out your feelings and fears.

Maggie's feelings of doubt combine with external demands on her to produce stress.

Maggie

Maggie was biting her nails again. What if Joe called? What would she say? How could she tell him that she wanted to stay just friends? "Ow!" she cried as her teeth hit flesh instead of nail. Maggie pulled her finger out of her mouth angrily and sat on her hand. She read her math homework for the zillionth time. Boy, she hated math. What did *equilateral* mean, anyway? This was hopeless! The phone rang, and Maggie's heart stopped. She breathed a sigh of relief as she heard her mother start chatting with a friend.

Maggie got up and went into the bathroom. She stared at herself in the mirror. Hair wasn't bad. Sweater looked good. But her skin! Ugh! Volcano face! Her skin would never clear up in time for Carla's party. And that was another thing. She still hadn't asked her parents if she could go to the party. She knew they didn't like Carla.

Maybe she'd pretend she had a baby-sitting job. No. They'd find out . . .

The phone rang again. "Maggie! It's Joe," called her mother. "But don't talk too long! Remember, you still have to clean the kitchen and your room." Maggie gripped the side of the bathroom sink. She imagined that she was small enough to hide in the drain. Small enough to ride a water droplet all the way out to the reservoir. Small enough to sail on a twig-and-leaf boat to a magical island where there was no math homework, no dirty dishes, no pimples, no parents to say *no* to parties, no Joes who were unhappy with just being friends.

Maggie's feelings are far from unusual. Everyday crises and demands can often feel stressful. But what feels stressful to one person may not to another person. Different situations are stressful for different people because we all have our own strengths and weaknesses and our own sense of what we can and cannot do well.

If Maggie felt she could tell Joe that she just wanted to be friends without hurting his feelings, she might welcome rather than fear his call. If she believed she would eventually solve the math problems, she might consider her homework an interesting challenge rather than a burden. If she were confident that she could get her parents' permission to go to

Carla's party, she might not feel so worried about asking them. But Maggie's own feelings of doubt combine with the external demands on her to produce stress.

Maggie's friend Carla breezes through the difficulties that stop Maggie cold. She's an A math student. She also feels very comfortable with boys. She can't understand why Maggie's so stressed out about talking to Joe. But if Carla isn't invited to the right parties or her boyfriend forgets to call, she freaks out. She worries that she's losing her popularity, a very stressful thought for her. Knowing what stresses *you* is the first step in learning to manage stress.

Maggie's friend Carla breezes through difficulties that stop Maggie cold.

Know Your Pressure Points

Pressure points are the demands in your daily life that leave you feeling stressed. Try this exercise to identify your own pressure points. Write this sentence starter at the top of a piece of paper: "I feel stressed when . . . " Then complete it with the first eight things that come to mind. Write exactly what comes to mind, no matter how silly it may seem. Psychologists Nathaniel and E. Devers Branden suggest that you do this exercise each night for six nights. Then, on the seventh night, complete this sentence starter: "I am becoming more aware that . . ." This sentence-starter activity can help you get to know your pressure points.

As important as knowing your pressure points is understanding why they stress you out. **Psychiatrist** John Livingstone points out that many teens are aware of the *external* pressures in their lives. But they may be less aware of the *internal* beliefs or expectations that often contribute to those pressures becoming stressful.

For example, Maggie may have felt so stressed about talking to Joe because she expects herself to please people. Two parts of herself—the part that wanted to please and the part that did not want to be Joe's girlfriend—were in conflict. Being aware of this conflict could help Maggie develop more realistic expectations and a strategy for solving the problem.

Maggie might work on changing the idea "I should be able to please everyone" to "I am someone who tries to please people, but I know this is sometimes impossible." She might work on becoming aware of the bodily tension she feels when she wants to please someone but can't. She could practice letting go of the feeling, imagining the tension running like rivers out of her fingertips. If she could do this, situations like the one she faced with Joe might become less stressful.

Maggie might also work on recognizing that she is not responsible for Joe's feelings. Her actions may trigger those feelings, but Joe, not Maggie, is responsible for them. He alone controls how he acts and feels. Many teens believe that they are responsible for other people's feelings, including their parents'. This sense of responsibility can add to their own feelings of stress.

One good way to become aware of the internal beliefs that contribute to your stress is to try **visualization**. Lie down or sit in a quiet place where you can relax. Close your eyes. Take a deep breath. Now imagine yourself in the situation that is causing you stress. Imagine the worst thing that could happen. Why is it so bad? How will you feel about yourself if it happens? Now imagine the best thing that could happen. Why is it good? How will you feel about yourself if it happens? How do your best and worst fantasies compare? What do they tell you about yourself? Keeping a diary or "thinking out loud" into a tape recorder is another good way to get to know your inner self.

Keeping a diary or "thinking out loud" into a tape recorder is another way to get to know your inner self.

Know Your Activity Type

"Let's see. After school today I've got wrestling practice and a meeting about this park cleanup project we've got going," says Juan. "Then I promised my dad I'd help stuff envelopes for this business thing he has to do. There's homework, and working out, and I want to have it all done before this movie I want to see comes on.

"It's my kind of day," Juan continues. "I love feeling pushed. It gives me an edge."

Mark is just the opposite. "I'm a very private person," he says, "and I like having a lot of time to myself. I get real tense when I have too much to do, too many people wanting things from me."

Neither Juan's nor Mark's style is wrong. People differ in the amount of pressure they can handle without feeling stressed. In fact, some researchers believe that people have a **genetic predisposition** to tolerate greater or lesser amounts of activity. Stress

How much activity do you prefer? Are you a curl-up-with-the-cat-and-enjoy-a-good-movie type of person?

comes, these researchers say, from a mismatch between an individual's **temperament** and his or her lifestyle. Mark could never enjoy Juan's schedule. On the other hand, living as quietly as Mark would be stressful for Juan. This doesn't mean that Mark couldn't learn to be a bit more outgoing, or that Juan can never enjoy quiet times. Temperament isn't cast in stone. It is shaped by our experiences. But a general tendency toward needing more or less stimulation may be inherited.

How much activity do you prefer? Are you a curl-up-with-the-cat-and-enjoy-a-good-movie type of person? Or are you a party animal, ready to go from morning to night? Think about the times you've felt happiest and most in control of your life. What were you doing? How much pressure were you under? How do those times compare to now? Like knowing your pressure points, knowing your activity type can help you make good choices for yourself.

Damien

While pressure points and activity type are different for different people, some events are stressful for anyone. Consider Damien's story.

Damien's family moved after his cousin Leroy became a headline. Leroy was a good kid standing on the wrong corner at the wrong time. Rumor was that the guy in the car, the guy who did the shooting, was aiming for Ramon, who was standing next to Leroy. But the bullet hit Leroy right in the head. "At least he didn't suffer," people said, trying to comfort the family.

Leroy wasn't the first kid Damien knew who was murdered. But he was the closest, and after it happened, Damien's mother asked her boss for a raise, got it, and moved the family to a new neighborhood. "I know it's safer here and everything," says Damien about his new home, "but I don't know anyone and the schoolwork's harder. I feel lost. I can't concentrate in school 'cause I keep thinking about Leroy. That could've been me, you know? So I should be happy I'm outta there, away from that neighborhood, right? But I'm not. I miss it. I miss my friends. I feel all messed up."

The death of a close relative, moving to a new neighborhood, and changing schools are what social scientists call **major life stresses**. They are events that would be difficult for anybody. The divorce of one's parents, getting in trouble with the law, and breaking up with a girlfriend or boyfriend are other major life events known to cause stress. So, too, are such positive events as receiving a special honor, starting a new job, or getting accepted to a team, club, or college.

Many major life stresses are difficult because they demand that we change and that we manage the feelings the changes bring. Damien must adjust to life in a new neighborhood. He needs to learn the ways of a new school, make new friends, prove himself to a new set of teachers who expect more of him than the teachers in his previous school did. The move from grade school to middle school or junior high is often stressful for many of the same reasons.

Adjusting to all of these changes will take time for Damien, as it would for anyone. So, too, will adjusting to life *without* a different source of stress—an unsafe neighborhood. "I still have my don't-mess-with-me walk," says Damien. "You know . . . arms tight, ready to fight,

Too many teens, like Damien, have had to adapt to the very real and difficult pressures of living with the fear of dying.

eyes dead ahead. People here don't walk that way. They don't have to."

Too many teens, like Damien, have had to adapt to the very real and difficult pressures of living with the fear of dying. They pass through metal detectors on their way into school and stare out classroom windows made of bulletproof glass. Their communities feel more like war zones than neighborhoods.

The pressures of living under such conditions are enormous, especially since most teens have so little control over the violence shaping their lives. Like Damien's cousin Leroy, they could someday be standing at the wrong place at the wrong time. The stress that situations like these cause can be overwhelming. So, too, can the stress that results from major life events. But you can take action to manage these feelings.

*Recognizing
what you can
and cannot
control, then
trying to change
what you can,
is one of the keys
to managing
stress that
comes from
living under
constant strain.*

Who's in Control?

Aphilosopher, Reinhold Niebuhr, once wished for the courage to change those things that he could, the serenity to accept those things that he could not change, and the wisdom to know the difference.

Recognizing what you can and cannot control, then trying to change what you can, is one of the keys to managing the stress that comes from experiencing major life changes or from living under constant strain. The threat of street violence is one type of constant strain. So, too, is living with an abusive relative or being the target of bullies at school.

What can teens control in such situations or when they are confronted with a major life change such as their parents' divorce? What is beyond our control? To begin with, we can rarely change other people's behavior. But we can change our own. We can't, for example, stop others from joining gangs and carrying guns. But we can choose not to do these things ourselves. We can heed the Reverend Jesse

Jackson's plea to "break the code of silence" and tell those in authority when we know who committed a crime. We can let the adults who are responsible for keeping us safe know that we need and expect their protection. We can learn about the things they are doing to try to make our lives safer.

We can walk with friends instead of alone and stay clear, as much as possible, of people we know to be violent. We can give ourselves permission *not* to worry about the things we can't control. The worry will contribute to our stress, but it will not change the situation. "You may not be able to control what happens," says psychiatrist John Livingstone, "but you can learn to control how you react to it."

When we change what we can change and accept what we cannot change, we take a big step toward reducing our stress. Our reality might not change at all. But our attitude toward it does, which makes the energy that stress gobbles up available for better uses.

In *The Wellness Book*, Dr. Herbert Benson recommends the following exercise for clearing your mind of worry and managing stress:

1. Stop yourself from thinking the worst. If, for example, your parents have just separated, you might fear that you will never see one of them again. When you find your thoughts spinning in this direction, say to yourself, "Stop the action," then move on to step 2.

2. Breathe deeply to let the physical tension out of your body. Breathe in through your nose to the count of 10. Then breathe out slowly through your mouth, also to the count of 10.

3. Reflect on the cause of your stress. What has happened to make you feel this way? What can you control in the situation? What can't you control?

4. Choose the way you will deal with the situation. If someone you love is very ill, for example, you may not be able to change the situation. But you can think of ways to show your love, or you can talk with someone you trust about the fear and pain you feel.

By taking action where you can, you will build a sense of personal control. And a feeling of personal control, studies show, is one of the keys to managing stress. If you are in a stressful situation that you cannot control, you may also benefit from taking on a new challenge or hobby. Stress researcher Suzanne Oullette Kobasa says that mastering a new skill can often reassure people that they can still cope. And commitment to enjoyable work or a hobby is another stress buster. Research suggests that people who really enjoy what they do are less likely to feel stressed, even when they're under great pressure. So make sure that any new activity you choose is consistent with your interests and abilities. You want it to reduce, not add to, the stress you feel!

Share the Feelings

Another activity that helps people deal with stressful feelings is talking. Remember Andy, the boy whose math teacher humiliated him in class? He finally told his father what was going on. Rather than feeling worse and embarrassed, as he'd expected, Andy felt better after talking. "It felt like this big weight was lifted off me," says Andy. "I didn't have this secret anymore, and my father didn't laugh at me or say that the math teacher was right, like I'd feared." Andy felt better even though the situation with his math teacher had not changed.

Stress research shows that people who have friends or family members they can turn to when the pressure's on get through stressful situations better than those who don't. Friends and family may be able to provide concrete support—running an errand for you when you don't have time, for example. But they don't

have to solve your problems to help. In fact, it's better if they don't. You're more in control when you solve your problems yourself, and personal control, as you know, helps you master stress. Ideally, family and friends should listen without judging or trying to fix the situation.

You can ask a parent or other adult or friend to listen. You can say, "I have some stuff I really need to work through. Could you help me by just listening without judging or trying to solve my problem?" Counselors can also help you sort through your feelings, especially if you feel so much stress that it is interfering with your life.

The healing power of human communication is amazing. The ability to communicate with other hostages was one of the things that enabled Terry Waite to survive his long and stressful ordeal of being held hostage in Lebanon from 1987 to 1991. Chained in their separate, solid-walled cells, the hostages could not hear one another's voices, so they could not talk. But they could tap on the walls. And they did, sending messages to each other. That tapping, that crude form of communication, became a lifeline.

Exercise,

especially

aerobic exercise,

helps release

the physical

tension that

builds up

when you

feel stressed.

Stressproofing Your Body

"When I feel stressed out, I try to go for a run," says Marion. "It feels great, and when I come back, I'm more relaxed, I have more energy, and things don't seem as bad."

Marion has hit on one of the major ways of effectively managing stress: exercise. Exercise, especially **aerobic exercise**, helps release the physical tension that builds up when you feel stressed.

You can stressproof your body in other ways, too. First, tune into your body. You might be so used to feeling stressed that you don't even recognize your body's warning signs. So do a stress check. Start at the top of your head and work down. Is your head aching? Is your neck stiff? Are your muscles tense? What's your body telling you? Once you know, you can try some of the following ideas for de-stressing. Choose the ones that work for you and try to make them part of your life.

■ *Breathe deep*. Deep breathing is a **relaxation technique**. Like exercise, it helps you calm a stressed-out body. Sit or lie down in a quiet, comfortable place. Close your eyes. Place a hand on your stomach. Now breathe in slowly through your nose. You should feel your stomach move up. Breathe out slowly through your mouth. You should feel your stomach go down. Continue your deep breathing until you feel more relaxed. **Meditation** and **progressive relaxation** are other relaxation techniques you can learn about and use to reduce stress. Listening to music is another good way to calm clamoring nerves.

■ *Eat well*. This advice may sound like something from your fourth-grade science book, but eating a balanced diet really is a good way to reduce stress. Your body needs a steady flow of energy, which you can get only from eating regularly. Your body also needs the nutrients that come with a balanced diet. The B vitamins (good sources include whole grains and leafy green vegetables) are especially linked to stress resistance. Vitamin A (found in yellow, orange, and dark green fruits and vegetables as well as dairy products) helps keep your immune system strong.

■ *Sleep well*. Tired bodies and sluggish brains can't respond quickly or creatively. They are more easily

If you don't have time to nap, at least take a little time out to relax.

stressed. Indeed, recent research suggests that a good night's sleep plus a short nap each day can help people do their best. If you don't have the time to nap, at least take a little time out to relax.

■ *Skip the caffeine.* And the alcohol or drugs or nicotine. Although some people use these substances to help reduce stress, they actually interfere with your body's ability to cope. And remember—cola and chocolate are prime sources of caffeine.

A stressproofed body contributes to stressproofing your mind. So does thinking about the way you think.

The Can't-Do-It, Sure-to-Fail, Why-Bother Blues

"**M**y science teacher assigned us lab partners. So who does she give me? Cindy, this girl I really like but who wouldn't even look at me if she didn't have to," says Kevin. "I can hardly talk to her. I mean, I want to, but she's so popular and everything and I'm . . . well, I'm not like that. The guys she hangs with are easy and funny, and me, I couldn't make her laugh if I were Jay Leno. I could never get her to like me."

Kevin might be right. He and Cindy might be so different that they wouldn't have much of a chance at romance, or even friendship. But the way he's thinking about Cindy pretty much guarantees that he won't have a chance to find out. What's more, Kevin's concerns make science class a torture. He feels so stressed out when he's around Cindy that his hands sweat and his throat goes dry. He can't even concentrate on his work.

Kevin may or may not be able to win Cindy's heart. But he can do a lot to lessen his stress. Researchers believe that the way we think about our problems contributes to how stressful they seem to us. Thoughts influence feelings as much as feelings influence thoughts. In fact, a special type of counseling called **cognitive therapy** helps people change their thoughts as a first step toward changing their moods and behavior.

Negative thoughts are like mental quicksand. They swallow up self-esteem. They make us feel less in control of our lives, more worried, more threatened, more stressed. Cognitive therapists suggest a triple-A program for changing negative thought habits: Become *aware* of the thought habits, *answer* them with more realistic, positive thoughts, and *act* on the positive responses.

Here are some thought traps to watch out for:

■ *Worst-case thinking.* "I'm going to fail the test, which means I'll fail the course and they'll throw me out of school." "If I don't make the team, I'll never play basketball again." Answer these negative thoughts with more realistic, positive ones: "I might not make the team now, but I can practice hard and try again next term."

■ *Jumping to conclusions.* "Jeff said he'd call but didn't. He must really hate me." Get the facts before you reach a conclusion. Does Jeff talk to you at school? Do any of your friends know how he feels about you? Can you ask him why he didn't call? Knowing the facts will help you evaluate the situation more realistically before you act.

■ *The "me" syndrome.* "Everyone saw me fall in the cafeteria. I'm so embarrassed!" Although we may think so, we're really not the center of the universe. Other people aren't waiting to catch our every mistake—or, for that matter, to applaud our every success. By turning off the spotlight, we can also turn off some of the pressure.

■ *Exaggerating.* "Everybody hates me." "I can't do anything right." "I'll never get invited to a party." Step back from such thoughts and do a reality check. Think about the incident that gave rise to the feeling. Now think about a similar time when things turned out differently—when you were invited to a party, for example.

Sometimes these thought traps and the feelings that accompany them are so much a part of us that we're not even aware of them. By becoming aware of our own patterns, answering them with more positive responses, and acting on the positive, we can make our thoughts become less stressful.

Time, Time, Time

Y ou've just sat down to write the book report due tomorrow when the phone rings. It's your best friend, who *has* to tell you about this call she just got from Joel, the guy she's had a crush on for two years. You listen, you talk, you share her excitement. Then you hang up and start thinking about Greg, the guy you wish would call you! Your kid brother interrupts your daydream. Could you help him with his math, please? How can you say no? You help with his homework, get a snack, then decide to watch just a few minutes of a new TV show. Before you know it, the show's over, it's nine o'clock, and you still haven't written the book report. You feel panic turning your stomach to mush. You'll never have enough time to finish the report now!

If this situation sounds familiar, take heart. Many teens experience stressful time crunches. Often we put off tasks we don't like. At other times we commit to too

You can learn techniques that can help you manage your time more efficiently. Planning and setting priorities are two of these.

much: Hockey practice, religious school, drama club, a part-time job, and a full load of schoolwork might compete for our time. We can also get into a crunch when we don't plan well enough.

Such problems are not unique to teens. So many adults have trouble organizing their time that businesses sometimes hire time management specialists to help their employees! Like these adults, you can learn techniques that can help you manage your time more efficiently. Not all of these suggestions work for all people. Try them. Then choose the ones that will work for you.

■ *Break large projects into small parts.* Sometimes a task seems so overwhelming that we think we'll never get it done. But any large job can be broken down into smaller tasks, and the smaller tasks are rarely as threatening as the whole. Then set a goal for completing each of the smaller tasks. Small goals are easier to meet. And meeting them will make you feel good. You might even consider rewarding yourself each time you do!

■ *Plan.* Read directions for projects and get all materials you need before you begin. Similarly, if you are planning a party, a trip, or some other big event, think through what you will need in advance. Make lists. Give yourself enough time to prepare. Get help if you need it.

■ *Set priorities.* Make a list of everything you need to do for the day. Then number your tasks in order of importance. Do the most important things first. If two tasks are equally important, do the one you *least* want to do first. That way it's over with, and you can reward yourself with a more enjoyable job.

■ *Do it!* You can tie yourself in knots worrying that you can't do something. Sometimes the best advice is to plunge in. And once you start, keep going. Put all your extra, stress-produced energy to good use!

■ *Learn to say no.* If you have too much to do, you may need to set limits for yourself. Make a list of all your commitments. Divide them into Have To's (homework, chores, and other responsibilities), Want To's (things you really want to do), and Would Rather Not's (things you've agreed to because you thought you should). Drop the Would Rather Not's. When new opportunities come up, evaluate them before saying yes. Make sure that you have the time *and* that you really want to take on the task.

Taking control of your time can help you take control of your life. And taking control of your life, as you now know, can help you manage stress.

A Final Word

This book has shared many ideas for managing stress in your life. Here's a brief recap.

■ *Feel smart.* Tune into your feelings so that you begin to recognize stress and the other emotions that may contribute to it. Accept that you are responsible for your feelings; other people are responsible for their own.

■ *Think smart.* Become aware of what's causing stress in your life. Think about your own beliefs and expectations, as well as about the changes you're going through and any outside pressures you face. Avoid the mental quicksand of negative thinking by becoming aware of your negative thoughts, answering them with more realistic ones, and acting on the positive responses.

■ *Talk smart.* Share your concerns with people you trust to listen without judging. Seek the social support that can help you through tough times.

■ *Act smart.* Take good care of your body by eating well, sleeping well, and exercising. Make relaxation exercises part of your routine. Get involved in activities you enjoy so that you can build some stress-beating success into your life. And take control of your time by planning, setting goals and priorities, and saying no.

And here's a final suggestion for managing your stressful feelings: laugh. It's hard to feel stressed when you're laughing. What's more, seeing the humor in a situation often puts your problems in perspective. They may not seem as bad. So turn on your favorite comedian. Call a friend who always cracks you up. Ask someone to tickle you. Laugh. It won't solve all your problems. But it will make them less stressful to bear.

Here's a final suggestion for managing stressful feelings: laugh. It's hard to feel stressed when you're laughing.

If You'd Like to Learn More

Organizations
The following groups provide information on stress.

American Institute of Stress
124 Park Avenue
Yonkers, NY 10703

The Hardiness Institute
19742 MacArthur Boulevard, Suite 100
Irvine, CA 92715-2408

Books
Books can help us understand our feelings better.
Here are some that deal with stress.

Changing Bodies, Changing Lives, by Ruth Bell
(New York: Random House, 1988). This thorough,
straightforward book about sexual development
answers questions about many topics that cause
teenagers to feel stressed.

*Don't Be S.A.D.: A Teenage Guide to Handling Stress,
Anxiety, and Depression*, by Susan Newman
(New York: Julian Messner, 1991). This book offers
first-person accounts by stressed-out teens, plus
strategies for those with similar problems.

Teenage Stress: How to Cope in a Complex World, by
Eileen Kalberg Van Wie (New York: Julian Messner,
1987). This look at personal, social, and environmental
stress includes exercises that can help readers identify
and rate the areas in their lives causing them stress.

Glossary/Index